Imagine...
Grover's Magic Carpet Ride

Featuring
Jim Henson's
Sesame Street
Muppets™

By Michaela Muntean
Illustrated by Tom Brannon

A SESAME STREET / GOLDEN BOOK

Published by Western Publishing Company, Inc., in conjunction with
Children's Television Workshop.

Sometimes I, Grover, pretend that the cute fuzzy carpet in my bedroom is not an ordinary carpet. I pretend it is a *magic* carpet.

Imagine . . . .

Whenever I want to go somewhere, all I have to do is sit on my carpet. I close my eyes and think hard about where I would like to go.

Then I open my eyes, and I am on my way. I am flying
through the air on a magic carpet ride!

I think I will visit my grandmother. Imagine her surprise
when I arrive at her house.

In the future, I must be more careful where I land. It can be very difficult for a little monster to get down from a roof.

There is room for two on my magic carpet, so I fly to Elmo's house and ask my friend if he wants to come along.

Of course he does. He makes some peanut butter and jelly sandwiches for the trip.

Elmo and I decide we want to go to the seashore.
When we both imagine, we get there twice as fast.

Oh, my goodness! I really must be careful where I land.
Now I have a soggy magic carpet.

While my magic carpet is drying in the sun, Elmo and I have time to go swimming . . .

and play on the beach.

The next place Elmo and I decide to go is Paris, France. I know it is a long way away, but we can be there in a jiffy on my magic carpet.

Across the ocean we fly! Far below we see white boats on the clear blue sea. Beneath us is my wonderful, magical carpet.

I think about what a lucky monster I am.

Up ahead we see the Eiffel Tower. It is much bigger than I thought.

There is no place to land a magic carpet, so around and around the tower we fly. Some little birdies come along for the ride.

Now we are flying higher than ever. Elmo and I lie back and enjoy the ride. Up through the clouds we go!

We fly to the top of a snowcapped mountain. It is cold, but my magic carpet helps keep us warm.

High above the countryside we fly! It is amazing how different everything looks from up here. Cows and horses and sheep look like tiny little toys.

As we fly over a city, the people on the ground look up and wonder what on earth is flying by. "Is it a bird?" they say. "Is it a plane?"

Soon I see Elmo's house. I swoop down and drop him off at his front door.

Now it is time for me to go home, too.

Oh, it is nice to be home again! It is nice to be in my
own little room with my own little bed and my own cute
little fuzzy magic carpet.